P9-DGT-847

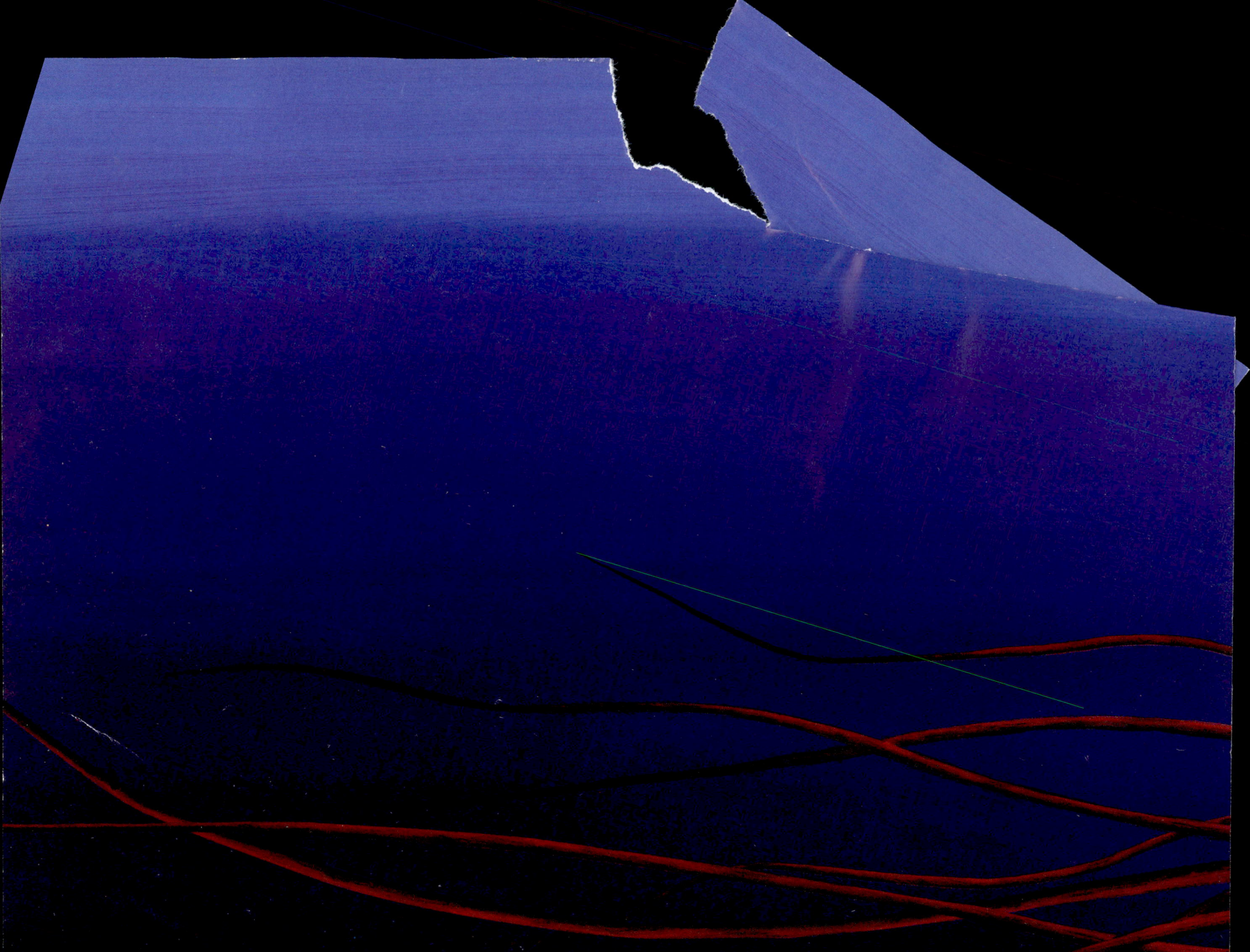

LEVEL 2 SCIENCE

LET'S READ AND FIND OUT

# HOW DEEP IS THE OCEAN?

BY KATHLEEN WEIDNER ZOEHFELD

ILLUSTRATED BY ERIC PUYBARET

HARPER

An Imprint of HarperCollinsPublishers

Special thanks to Dr. David Gruber, a marine biologist at the City University of New York and the American Museum of Natural History, for his valuable assistance.

The Let's-Read-and-Find-Out Science book series was originated by Dr. Franklyn M. Branley, Astronomer Emeritus and former Chairman of the American Museum of Natural History–Hayden Planetarium, and was formerly co-edited by him and Dr. Roma Gans, Professor Emeritus of Childhood Education, Teachers College, Columbia University. Text and illustrations for each of the books in the series are checked for accuracy by an expert in the relevant field. For more information about Let's-Read-and-Find-Out Science books, write to HarperCollins Children's Books, 195 Broadway, New York, NY 10007, or visit our website at www.letsreadandfindout.com.

Let's Read-and-Find-Out Science® is a trademark of HarperCollins Publishers.

How Deep Is the Ocean?

Text copyright © 2016 by Kathleen Weidner Zoehfeld
Illustrations copyright © 2016 by HarperCollins Publishers
All rights reserved. Manufactured in China.
No part of this book may be used or reproduced in any manner whatsoever without written permission except in the case of brief quotations embodied in critical articles and reviews. For information address HarperCollins Children's Books, a division of HarperCollins Publishers, 195 Broadway, New York, NY 10007.
www.harpercollinschildrens.com

Library of Congress Cataloging-in-Publication Data
Zoehfeld, Kathleen Weidner, author.
How deep is the ocean? / by Kathleen Weidner Zoehfeld ; illustrated by Eric Puybaret. — First edition.
pages cm — (Let's-read-and-find-out, Level 2)
ISBN 978-0-06-232820-5 (hardcover) — ISBN 978-0-06-232819-9 (pbk.)
1. Oceanography—Juvenile literature. 2. Ocean—Juvenile literature. 3. Children's questions and answers.
I. Puybaret, Eric, illustrator. II. Title.
GC21.5.Z64 2016 2015018471
551.46—dc23 CIP
AC

The artist used acrylic on paper to create the illustrations for this book.
Typography by Erica De Chavez
16 17 18 19 20 SCP 10 9 8 7 6 5 4 3 2 1
❖
First Edition

R0445941758

*For Brian*—K.Z.

*For Antoine and Claude*—E.P.

At the beach, it's fun to splash and play in the ocean waves. Seashells sparkle in the sunlight. Seaweed gets tangled in your toes.

You can watch your feet wiggling in the water as you wade out. Ankle-deep! Knee-deep! Waist-deep!

Look into the distance, and there's ocean as far as you can see.

Ocean covers almost three-quarters of the Earth. Near the shore, the water can be shallow enough for wading. But as you go farther out, it gets deeper and deeper.

If you want to explore the deep water, you're going to need some **scuba** gear!

You put on a waterproof mask so you can see underwater. You strap an air tank on your back for breathing and fins on your feet to help you swim faster. You dive down. The water is blue and lit by the sun above. You see fish and crabs, snails and clams, and so much more!

Hoses bring air from your air tank to your mouthpiece.

# YOU ARE IN THE SUNLIGHT ZONE.

All this colorful life depends on the plants of the sea—the seaweed that grows near shore and the tiny **phytoplankton** that float and swim in the open water.

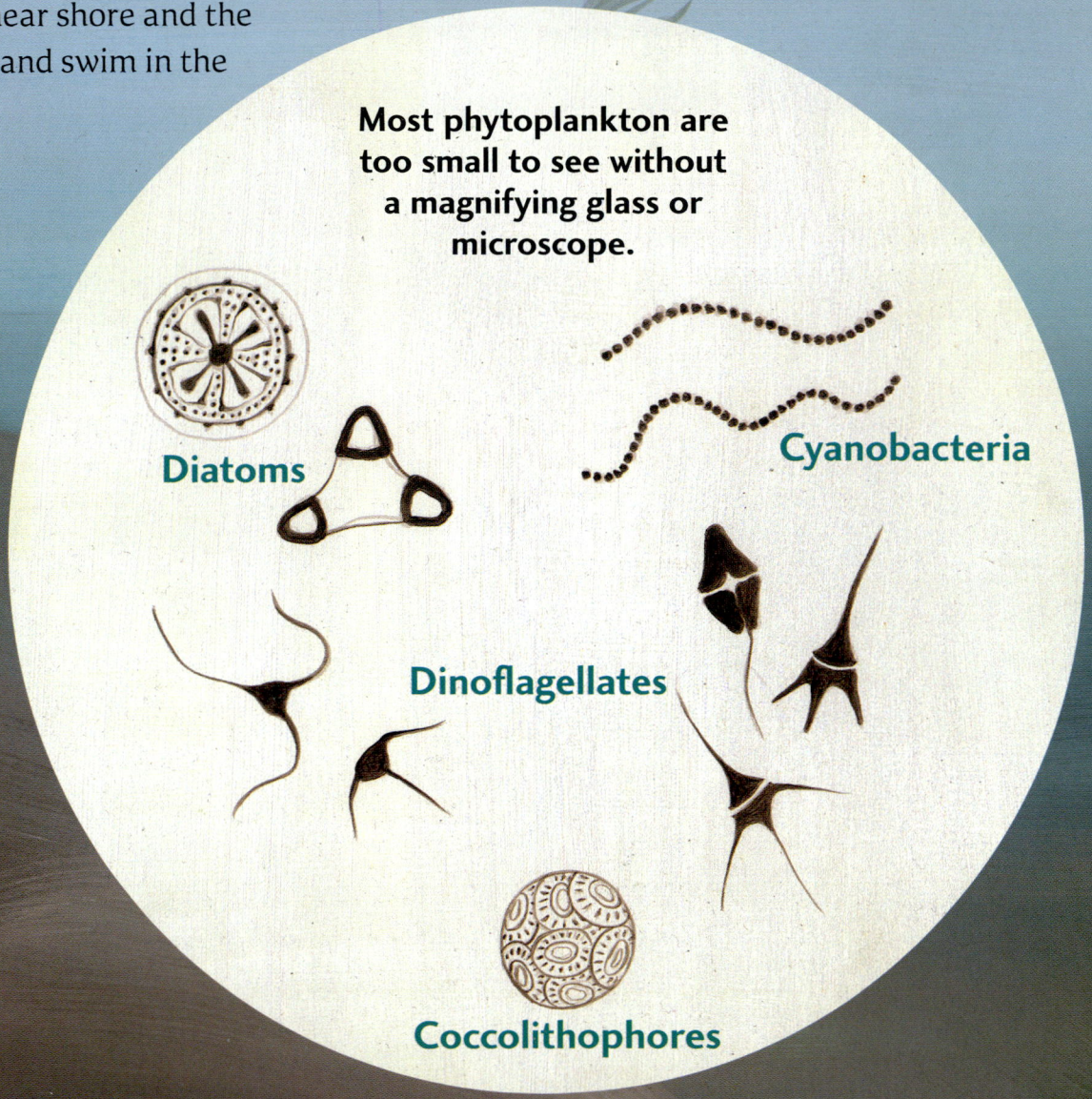


Kelp greenling

Garibaldi

Just like plants on land, sea plants use the energy of sunlight to make food. This process is called **photosynthesis**. Sea plants themselves are the food for countless kinds of sea animals.

## OCEAN DEPTH CHART:

0 to 328 feet (0 to 100 meters):
THE SUNLIGHT ZONE

328 to 3,300 feet (100 to 900 meters):
THE TWILIGHT ZONE

3,300 to 13,100 feet
(900 to 4,000 meters):
THE MIDNIGHT ZONE

13,100 to 19,700 feet
(4,000 to 6,000 meters)
THE ABYSSAL ZONE

19,700 to 36,188 feet
(6,000 to 11,030 meters)
THE HADAL ZONE

0
100
900
4,000
6,000
11,000

You kick your fins and swim deeper. About one hundred feet (30 meters) down, you may notice it's getting darker. The sun looks like a lamp far overhead.

At the beach, the water felt warm on your toes. Here, the water feels much colder. This far down, the pressure of the water on your body is getting uncomfortable, too. Water is much heavier than air. You can feel the water squeezing you. You feel it most in your ears and chest. Scuba divers rarely dive deeper than 130 feet (40 meters). That's about as deep as a twelve-story building is tall. Beyond that, the pressure becomes almost too great for humans.

Expert science divers use special equipment to swim down as far as 500 feet (150 meters). At that depth, you will see hardly any plants. Phytoplankton struggle to live in this dim environment. With only a little sunlight, photosynthesis becomes almost impossible. With few plants to feed on, there are fewer fish and other animals.

If you want to see what lives deeper than 500 feet, you'll have to climb aboard a **submersible**. It has strong metal sides to withstand high pressure. It's heated to keep you warm. And it carries air, so you can breathe.

Safe in your submersible, you dive down, down, down. Outside your window, you see only inky darkness. Hardly any sunlight can reach this far through the water.

**YOU HAVE REACHED THE TWILIGHT ZONE.**

You turn on your searchlight and scan for any sign of life. You spot a few jellyfish. Below 660 feet (200 meters), many animals have jelly-like bodies. Jelly animals are nearly invisible in the dim light here. This helps them hide from enemies or sneak up on prey.

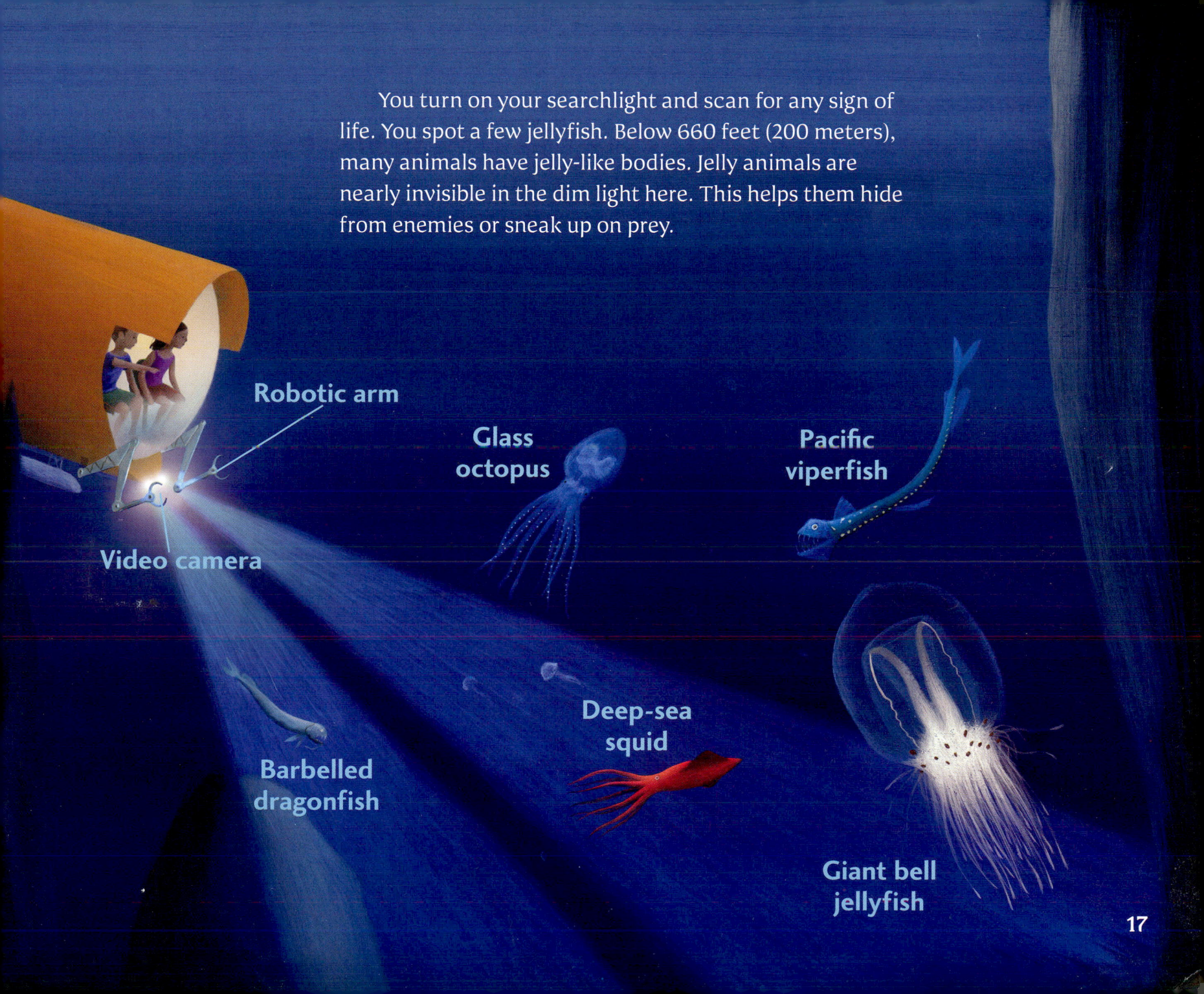

Some of the biggest animals in the world live down here too. Giant squid prowl the deep. They use their long tentacles to grab fish. A squid as long as a school bus looks pretty scary. But something even bigger hunts for them. The sperm whale—the largest predator in the world!

The giant squid has the largest eyes of any animal on the planet. Those big eyes may help the squid spot its enemy in the dim light.

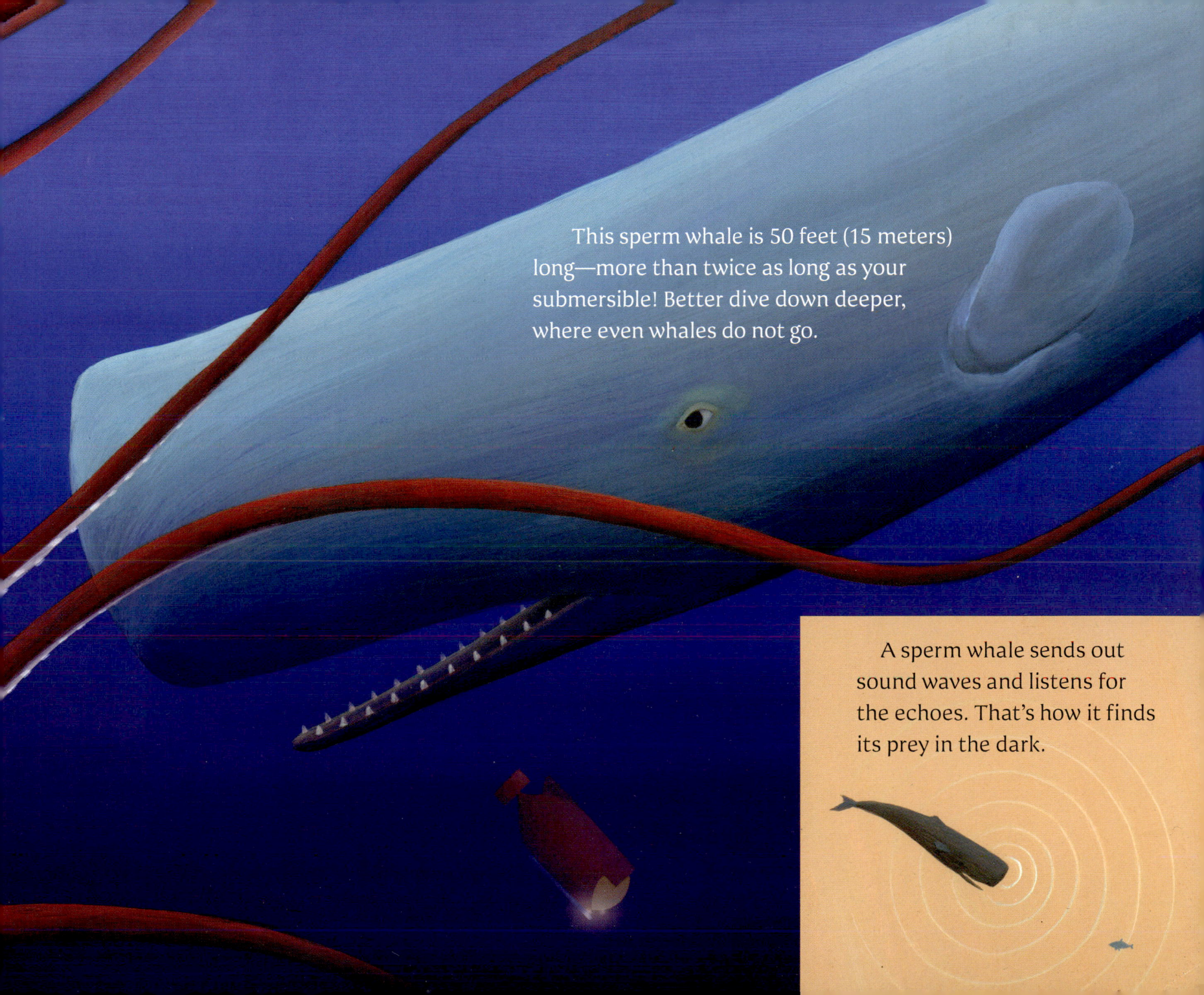

This sperm whale is 50 feet (15 meters) long—more than twice as long as your submersible! Better dive down deeper, where even whales do not go.

A sperm whale sends out sound waves and listens for the echoes. That's how it finds its prey in the dark.

# ENTERING THE MIDNIGHT ZONE

Around 3,300 feet (1,000 meters)—just over half a mile down—there is no light at all. Before the first submersible was invented, scientists weren't sure if anything could live for long in such darkness. But now we know many types of creatures are at home here.

Although there's no sunlight, there is animal light—or **bioluminescence**. On land, fireflies and glowworms make their own light. Here, thousands of different types of fish, jellies, shrimps, octopuses, and other animals do.

When night falls, many of them swim up toward the surface, where there is more food. Some, like the lanternfish, turn on their lights to find their food. They turn off their lights to hide from enemies.

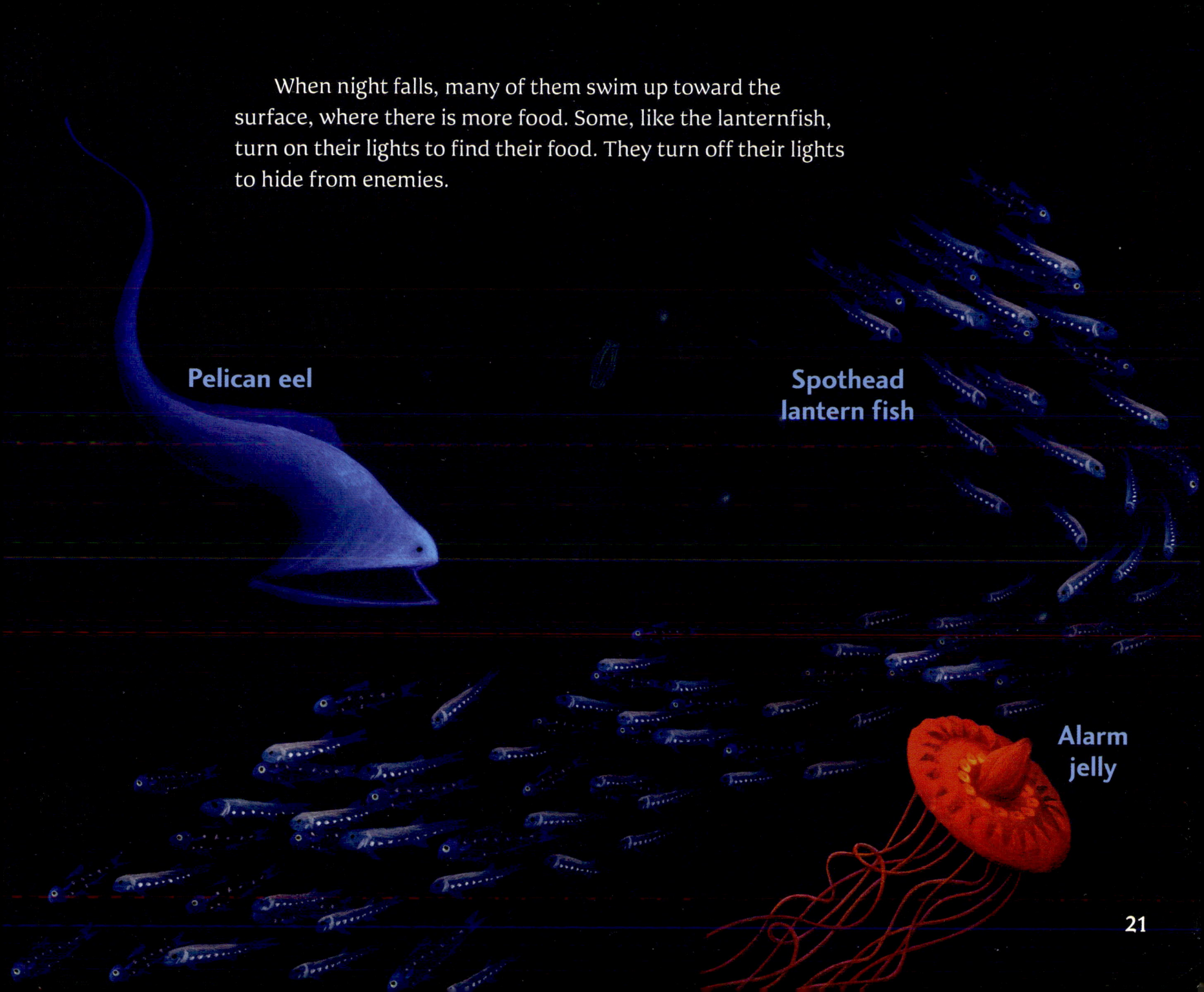

You take your submersible down even farther. At around two and a half miles (4,000 meters) deep, you see a muddy plain below you. You have reached the bottom. Scientists call it the Abyss.

The deep ocean floor makes up more than half of the Earth's surface. But we know very little about this area. More people have traveled into outer space than have been down this far.

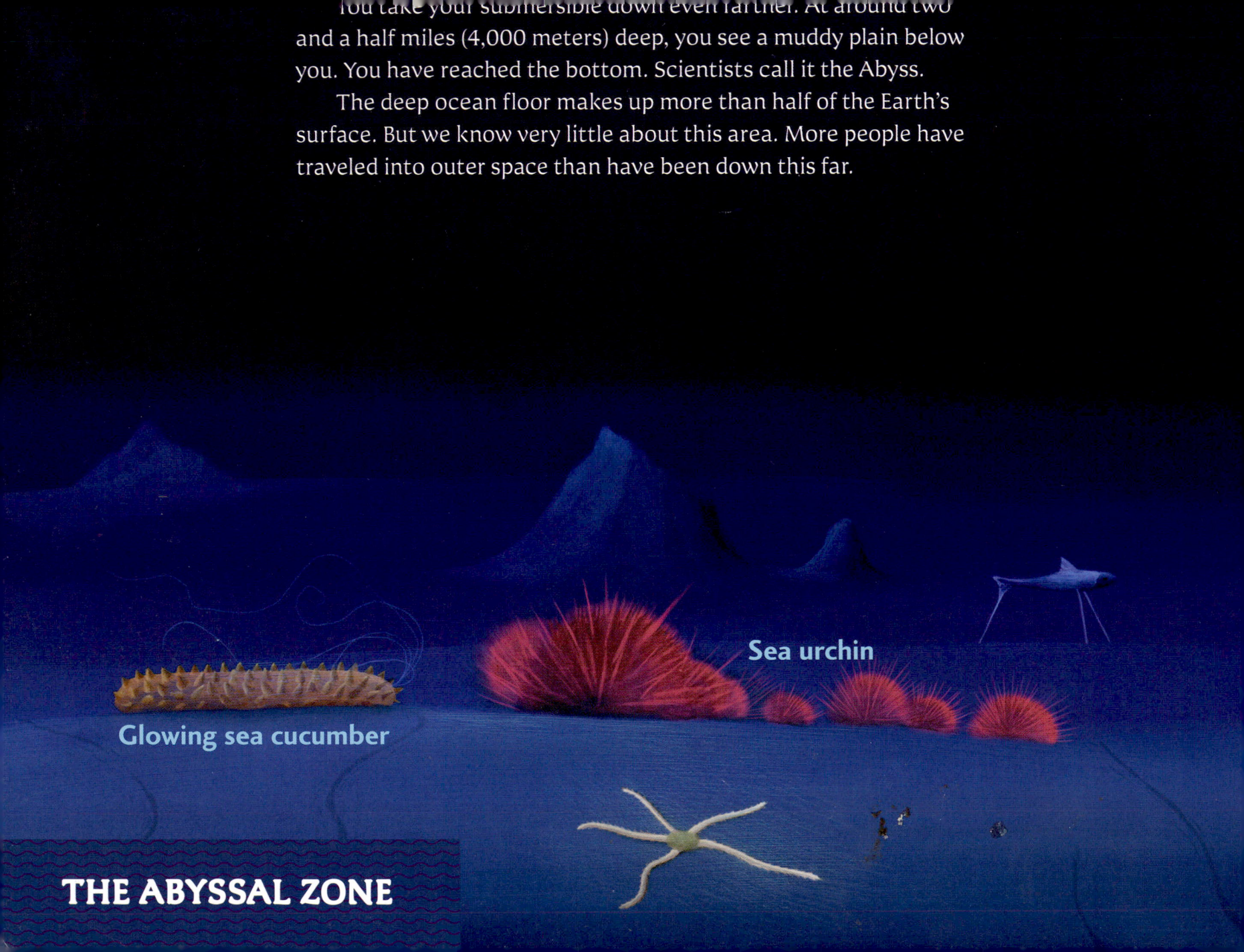


## THE ABYSSAL ZONE

At first it looks like there are no animals here. But look closely and you see tracks and trails everywhere. Brittle stars, sea urchins, and sea cucumbers crawl over the mud. They eat tiny particles of dead plants and animals that have drifted down from above.

You glide over the seafloor, scanning with your searchlight. There are many tracks but only a few animals. Each animal wanders far to find enough food in the mud.

Giant tube worms
Deep-sea vent crab
Hydrothermal sea snail

Then you spot what looks like smoke rising from a chimney. You steer your submersible in that direction. When you get close, you see a group of giant tube worms around the chimney. The worms are white, with red plumes on top. Some of them are more than six feet (two meters) long. There are many other animals crowded around them. This looks like an oasis in the desert!

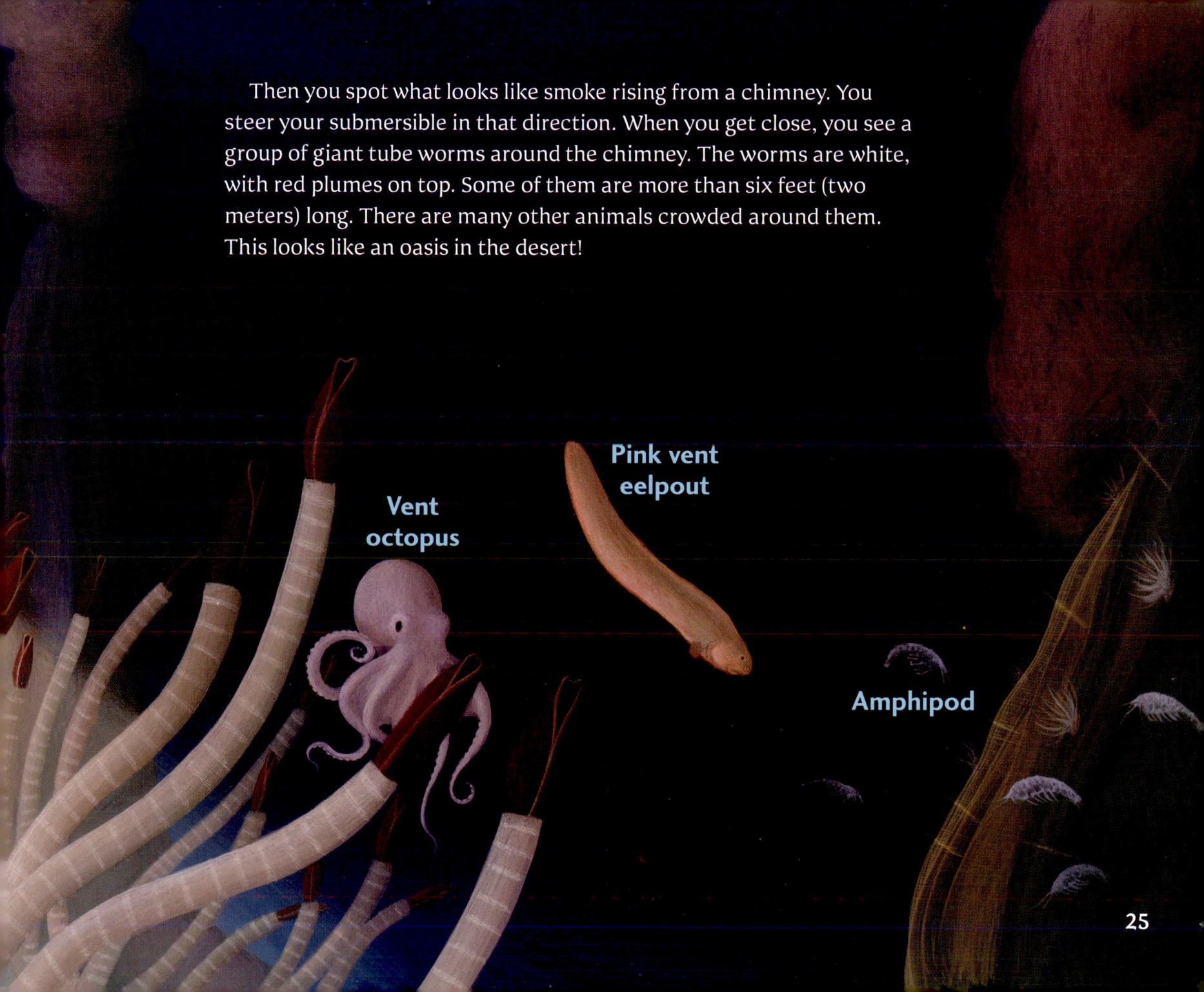

The smoking "chimney" is called a **hydrothermal** vent. In certain areas of the ocean floor, cold seawater seeps down through cracks. The water comes into contact with hot rock deep inside the Earth. The water heats up quickly. Minerals from the rock combine with the water. The hot, mineral-rich water shoots up through the cracks, like water volcanoes.

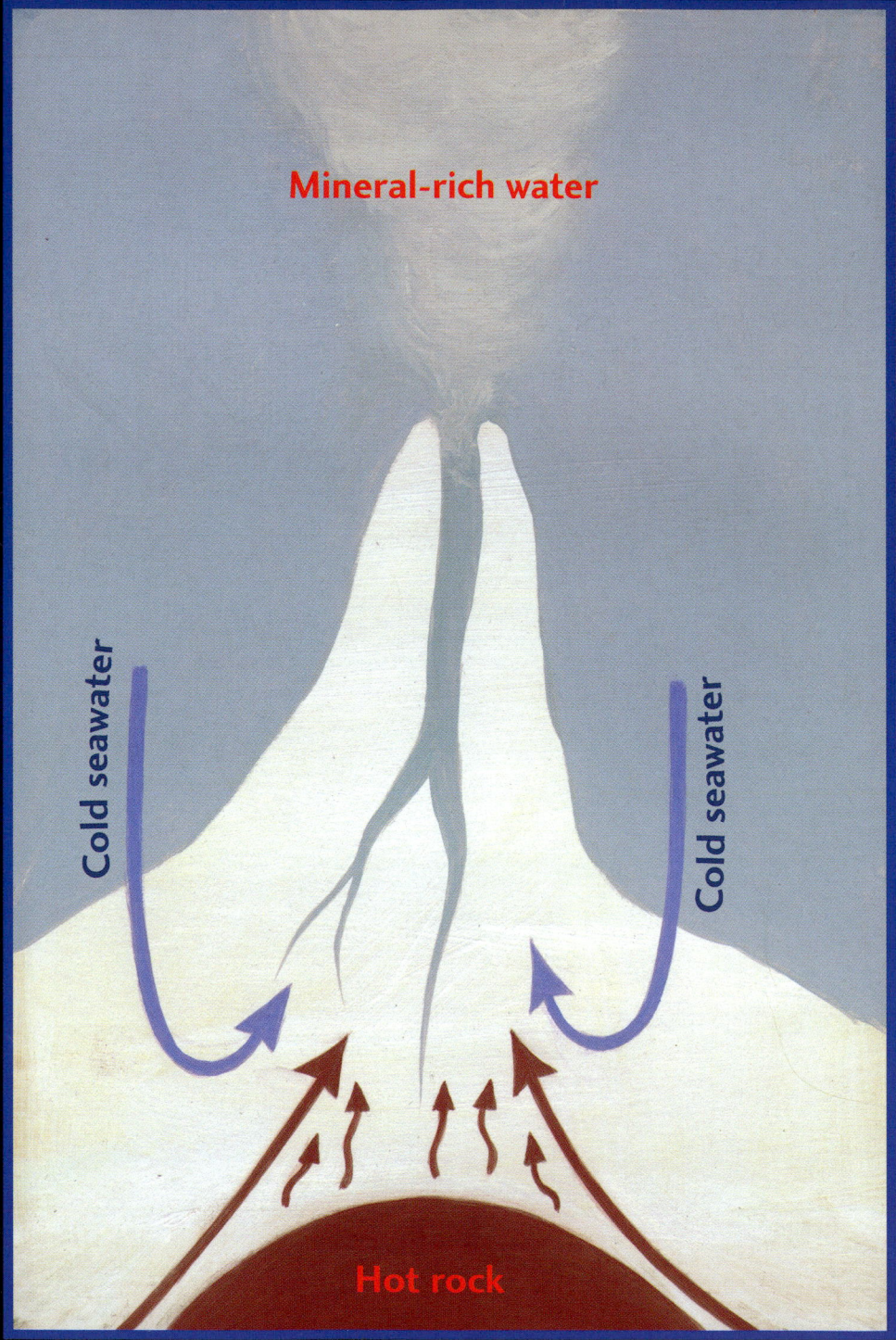

The water can be black or white, and it billows up like smoke. The minerals in the water slowly settle out to build tall cones that look like chimneys. When scientists first discovered the animals living around hydrothermal vents, it was like discovering life on another planet!

Scientists long thought that all life depended on light from the sun. Without it, there would be no photosynthesis. Without photosynthesis there could be no food, and no living things could survive. Yet here were animals living in total darkness, without using even a scrap of food from above. How could they possibly do it?

The tube worms here shelter huge numbers of **bacteria**. The worms use their red plumes to soak up a special chemical called **hydrogen sulfide** from the hot seawater. This chemical would be deadly for most living things. But these strange bacteria thrive on it. They use its energy to make food the worms can live on. This process is called **chemosynthesis**.

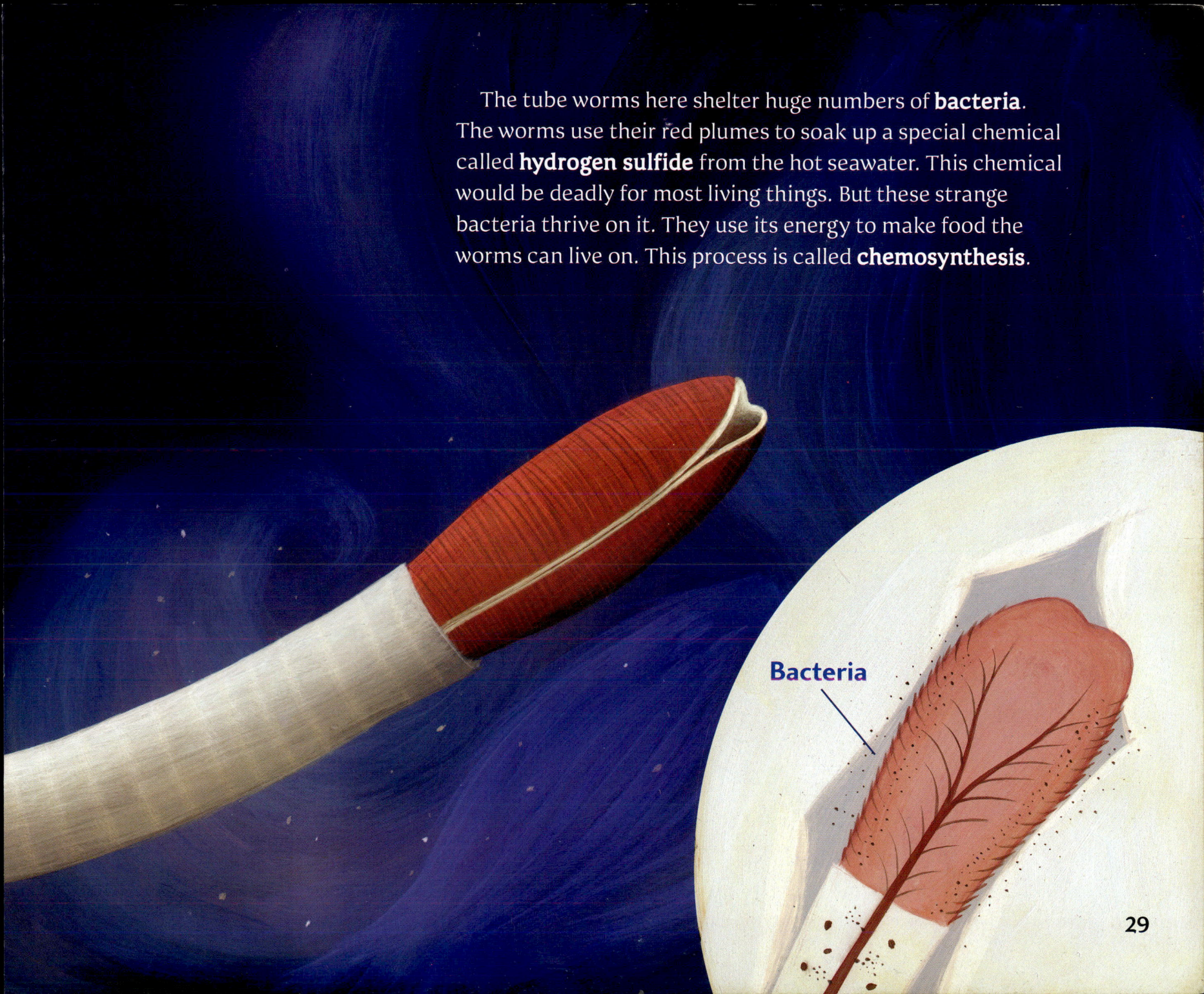

Small shrimp-like animals like to eat the bacteria, too. Many larger animals come to feed on the small animals. You see strange-looking fish, clams, snails, and crabs. Many look something like animals you are familiar with—but not quite!

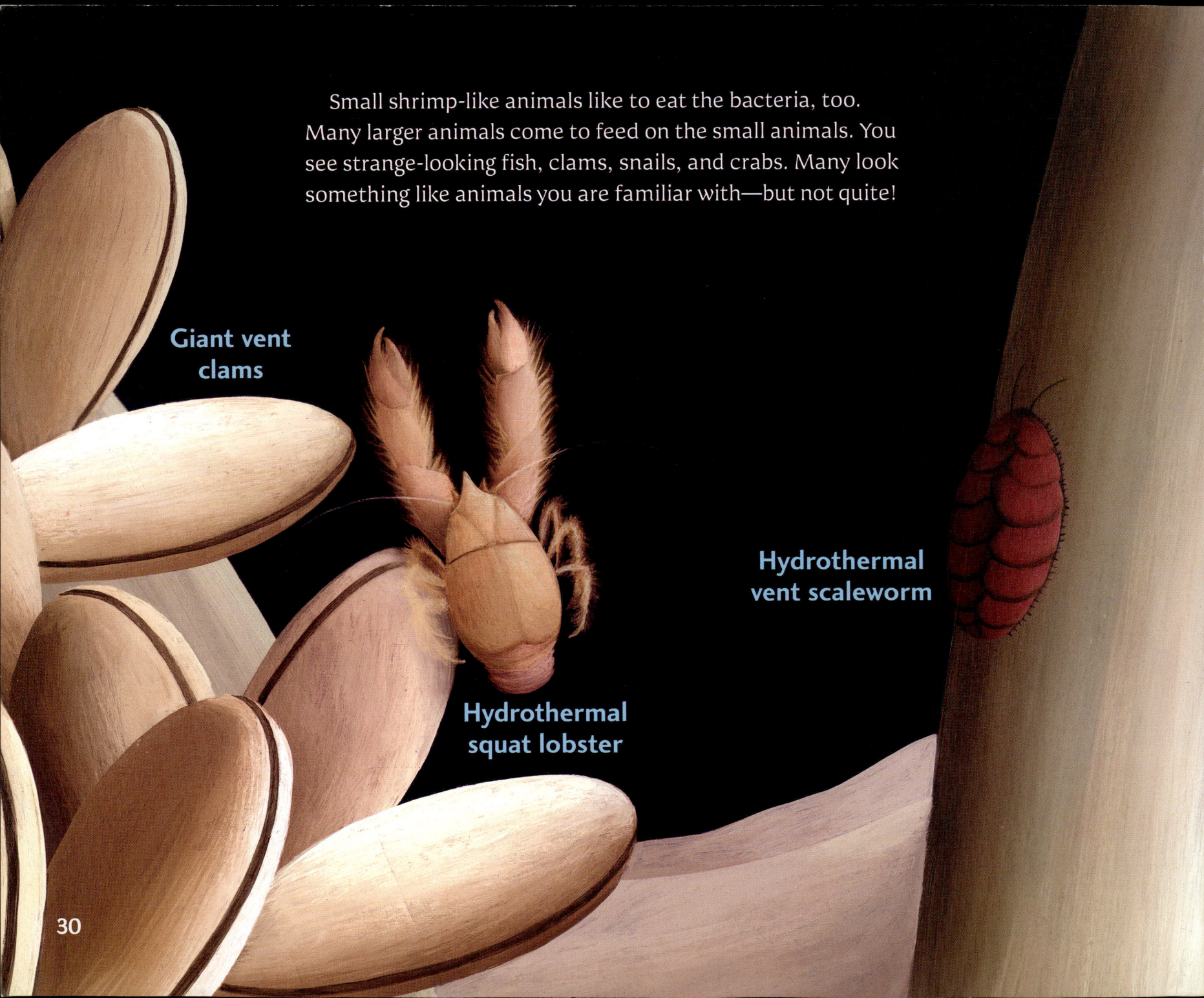

You've traveled more than three and a half miles (6,000 meters) to get here. You've seen many weird and wonderful sights. But there are even deeper, more mysterious places to see.

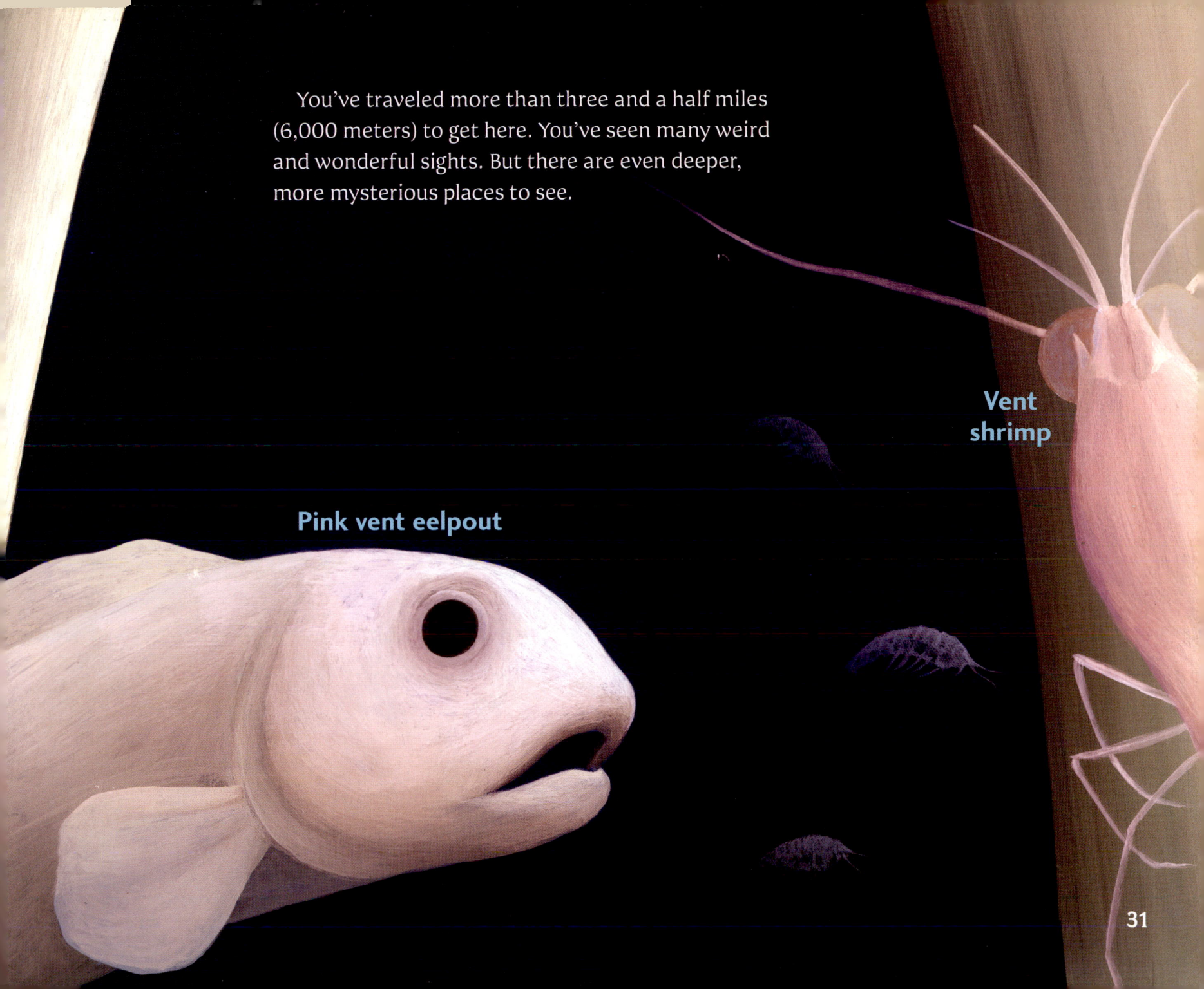

# THE HADAL ZONE

Crisscrossing the ocean are canyons so deep, they would make the Grand Canyon look tiny. The deepest of all is the Mariana Trench, in the western Pacific Ocean. The Grand Canyon is a little over one mile (1,830 meters) deep. The deepest part of the Mariana Trench reaches down nearly seven miles (11,030 meters)!

Are you ready to dive in? Only a few people have ever taken this journey. As you go, keep a sharp eye out for any signs of life. Scientists using deep-sea cameras have filmed odd kinds of fish, shrimp, sea cucumbers, and more! Even in the deepest, darkest, coldest depths of the ocean, there is life.

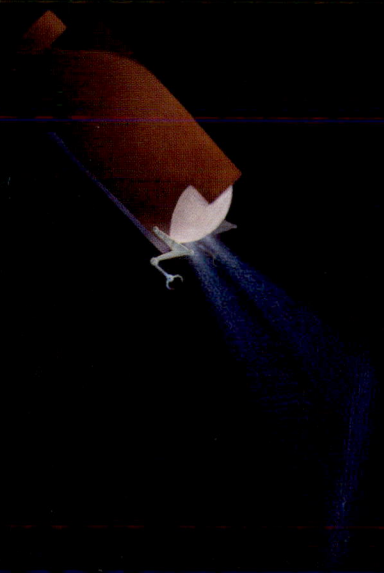

## Under Pressure!

When you are standing on the beach, you have about 15 pounds of pressure per square inch on your body. You are not underwater, but you are under air! It's called "one atmosphere" of pressure. And you don't feel it at all. It's what you're used to. For every 33 feet (10 meters) you dive down underwater, the pressure increases by one atmosphere.

Imagine trying to stand at the bottom of the Mariana Trench! There the pressure is more than 16,000 pounds per square inch. How do the animals that live there stand it? The pressure inside their bodies is the same as the pressure outside.

You can feel how even a little bit of water exerts some pressure.

To find out, you'll need:

- A long, narrow plastic bag, such as a bread bag
- A large, thick rubber band
- A large bowl of water, or sink, about half full of water

Slip your arm inside the bag. Use the rubber band to seal the top of the bag around your forearm, near your elbow. Then put your arm completely underwater. What happens to the bag? How does it feel?

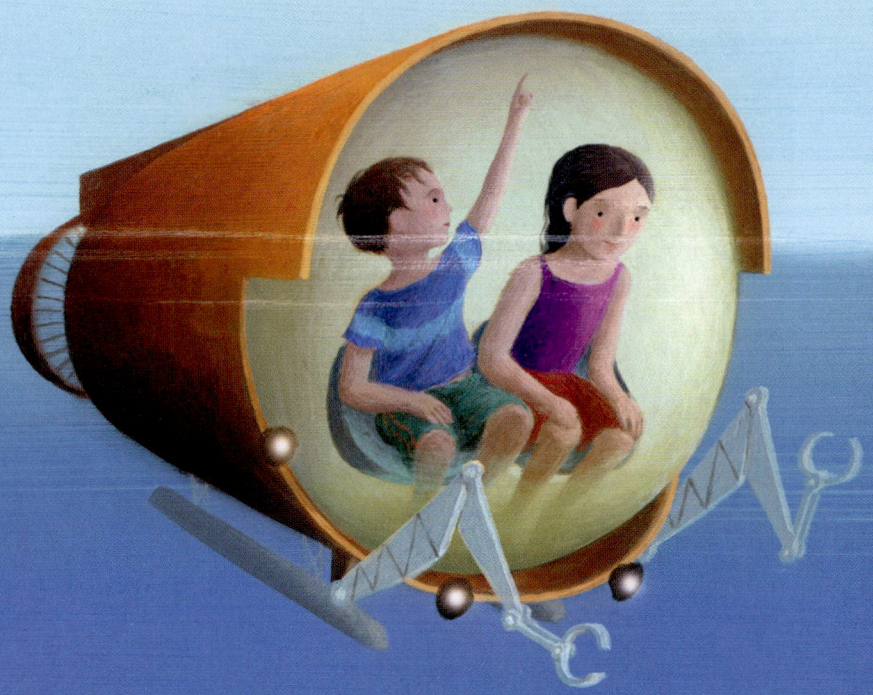

No doubt there are many new life-forms to be discovered here. But it's time to head home. You rise up—from the darkest depths to the sparkling sunlit surface. It has been a long trip, with many amazing sights along the way. Those who go down in submersibles never forget this strange and alien world. But it always feels good to come up into the sunlight again. Back where there's air to breathe, and the pressure is just right for humans!

# GLOSSARY

**Bacteria** (back-TEER-ee-uh): Tiny, single-celled organisms that live everywhere on Earth. There are millions of different kinds of bacteria.

**Bioluminescence** (BY-oh-LOO-mih-NESS-ents): The production of light by a living thing. Unlike light from the sun or other sources, this is usually a light without heat, or "cold light."

**Chemosynthesis** (KEE-moh-SIN-thu-sis): The process of making food from carbon dioxide and water, using energy from chemicals rather than the energy of the sun.

**Hydrogen sulfide** (HI-dro-gin SUL-fide): A colorless gas with the foul odor of rotten eggs. It often occurs with volcanic gasses, and it is easily set on fire and burns quickly.

**Hydrothermal** (HI-dro-THER-mul): Having to do with water heated by the energy of the Earth. From the Greek words *hydro* (or *hydor*), meaning "water," and *thermos*, meaning "heat."

**Photosynthesis** (FOE-toe-SIN-thu-sis): The process of making food from carbon dioxide and water, using energy from sunlight.

**Phytoplankton** (FY-toh-PLANK-ton): A vast multitude of tiny living things float, drift, or swim in the ocean's currents. These are called plankton. Phtyoplankton are plankton that make their own food, through photosynthesis.

**Scuba** (SKOO-bah): Short for: *S*elf-*c*ontained *u*nderwater *b*reathing *a*pparatus. Scuba gear lets divers breathe air while swimming underwater.

**Submersible** (sub-MER-si-bul): A small boat or craft especially made to travel underwater. Submersibles are used for deep-sea research.

# FIND OUT MORE ABOUT

## How to Measure the Deep Dark Sea

The ocean floor was once thought to be just a flat, muddy plain. We now know it's crisscrossed by deep trenches and high mountain ranges. But how did we find out? In 1872, Charles Wyville Thomson, chief scientist aboard the HMS (Her Majesty's Ship) *Challenger*, used a process called "sounding" to measure the ocean's depth at many different locations. You can make your own sounding line to see how it is done.

You'll need:

- A piece of string, about two feet (61 centimeters) long
- A metal washer
- A ruler
- A large bowl of water, or sink filled with water

1. Tie the metal washer to one end of the string. Then, tie a small knot one inch (2.5 centimeters) above the washer. Continue tying knots in the string, spacing them evenly—one inch apart. Use your ruler to make sure your spaces are exact.
2. Toss the washer overboard! And let it sink to the bottom of your bowl of water. Hold the other end of the string up straight. How many inches deep is the water in your bowl? Gently make waves in the water with your hand. What happens to your depth measurement? Does it change?

When participating in activities in this book, it is important to keep safety in mind. Children should always ask permission from an adult before doing any of the activities and should be supervised by an adult at all times. The publisher, author, and artist disclaim any liability from any injury that might result from the participation, proper or improper, of the activities contained in this book.

The *Challenger* scientists used rope and a heavy lead weight instead of string and a washer. They tied their knots every six feet (1.8 meters). That unit of measurement is called a "fathom." They were stunned to find a part of the ocean that was 26,850 feet (8,262 meters), or 4,475 fathoms, deep. (That's a LOT of rope!) They had discovered the Mariana Trench! The deepest part of the Trench is named "Challenger Deep" in their honor.

Today, scientists use sonar to measure the ocean's depths. A sonar device sends a sound wave, or "ping," down through the water. Sound travels through water at a constant rate. The sonar device records the time it takes for the ping to reach the seafloor and bounce, or echo, back. From that information, the scientists can calculate the exact depth of the water in that place.

## Hydrothermal vents and cold seeps

www.mbari.org/benthic/coldseeptour.htm

wwf.panda.org/about_our_earth/blue_planet/deep_sea/vents_seeps/

## Submersibles, ROVs, and Landers

www.oceanexplorer.noaa.gov/technology/subs/subs.html

www.ocean.si.edu/ocean-news/submarines-robots-exploring-deep-ocean

www.whoi.edu/hades/hadal-lander-b/

Please note that all of the websites mentioned are independent from HarperCollins Publishers, and HarperCollins, Kathleen Zoehfeld, and Eric Puybaret are not responsible for any problems arising out of use of, reference to, or communication with the websites. Ask your parents before visiting any website.

This book meets the Common Core State Standards for Science and Technical Subjects. For Common Core resources for this title and others, please visit www.readcommoncore.com.

# Be sure to look for all of these books in the Let's-Read-and-Find-Out Science series:

LEVEL 1

**The Human Body:**
How Many Teeth?
I'm Growing!
My Feet
My Five Senses
My Hands
Sleep Is for Everyone
What's for Lunch?

**Plants and Animals:**
Animals in Winter
Baby Whales Drink Milk
Big Tracks, Little Tracks
Bugs Are Insects
Dinosaurs Big and Small
Ducks Don't Get Wet
Fireflies in the Night
From Caterpillar to Butterfly
From Seed to Pumpkin
From Tadpole to Frog
How Animal Babies Stay Safe
How a Seed Grows
A Nest Full of Eggs
Starfish
A Tree Is a Plant
What Lives in a Shell?
What's Alive?
What's It Like to Be a Fish?
Where Are the Night Animals?
Where Do Chicks Come From?

**The World Around Us:**
Air Is All Around You
The Big Dipper
Clouds
Is There Life in Outer Space?
Pop!
Snow Is Falling
Sounds All Around
The Sun and the Moon
What Makes a Shadow?

LEVEL 2

**The Human Body:**
A Drop of Blood
Germs Make Me Sick!
Hear Your Heart
The Skeleton Inside You
What Happens to a Hamburger?
Why I Sneeze, Shiver, Hiccup, and Yawn
Your Skin and Mine

**Plants and Animals:**
Almost Gone
Ant Cities
Be a Friend to Trees
Chirping Crickets
Corn Is Maize
Dolphin Talk
Honey in a Hive
How Do Apples Grow?
How Do Birds Find Their Way?
Life in a Coral Reef
Look Out for Turtles!
Milk from Cow to Carton
An Octopus Is Amazing
Penguin Chick
Sharks Have Six Senses
Snakes Are Hunters
Spinning Spiders
Sponges Are Skeletons
What Color Is Camouflage?
Who Eats What?
Who Lives in an Alligator Hole?
Why Do Leaves Change Color?
Why Frogs Are Wet
Wiggling Worms at Work
Zipping, Zapping, Zooming Bats

**Dinosaurs:**
Did Dinosaurs Have Feathers?
Digging Up Dinosaurs
Dinosaur Bones
Dinosaur Tracks
Dinosaurs Are Different
Fossils Tell of Long Ago
My Visit to the Dinosaurs
What Happened to the Dinosaurs?
Where Did Dinosaurs Come From?

**Space:**
Floating in Space
The International Space Station
Mission to Mars
The Moon Seems to Change
The Planets in Our Solar System
The Sky Is Full of Stars
The Sun
What Makes Day and Night
What the Moon Is Like

**Weather and the Seasons:**
Down Comes the Rain
Feel the Wind
Flash, Crash, Rumble, and Roll
Hurricane Watch
Sunshine Makes the Seasons
Tornado Alert
What Will the Weather Be?

**Our Earth:**
Archaeologists Dig for Clues
Earthquakes
Follow the Water from Brook to Ocean
How Deep Is the Ocean?
How Mountains Are Made
In the Rainforest
Let's Go Rock Collecting
Oil Spill!
Volcanoes
What Happens to Our Trash?
What's So Bad About Gasoline?
Where Do Polar Bears Live?
Why Are the Ice Caps Melting?
You're Aboard Spaceship Earth

**The World Around Us:**
Day Light, Night Light
Energy Makes Things Happen
Forces Make Things Move
Gravity Is a Mystery
How People Learned to Fly
Light Is All Around Us
Switch On, Switch Off
What Is the World Made Of?
What Makes a Magnet?
Where Does the Garbage Go?